This Little Tiger book belongs to:

_____

_____

_____

For Jazz

~ J. T.

LITTLE TIGER PRESS
1 The Coda Centre, 189 Munster Road,
London SW6 6AW
www.littletiger.co.uk

First published in Great Britain 2003
by Little Tiger Press, London
This edition published 2012

Printed in China • LTP/1900/0833/0913

2 3 4 5 6 7 8 9 10

Andrew Murray

The Very Sleepy Sloth

Jack Tickle

LITTLE TIGER PRESS

Deep in the jungle,
early in the morning,
the sloth was fast asleep.

But the rest of
the animals were
wide awake.

The cheetah was on the treadmill, working on his

SPEED.

The elephant was lifting heavy weights, working on her

STRENGTH.

The kangaroo was
on the trampoline,
working on her

SPRING.

The monkey was
on the high bars,
working on his

SWING.

While the sloth stayed
in his hammock,
working on his sleep.

"That sloth is so lazy,"
said Cheetah.

"All he does is lie there!"
agreed Elephant.

"Just dozing in his hammock,"
added Kangaroo.

"Hey, Sloth!" called Monkey.
"We're all working hard here.
Why don't you get up and
do something?"

Sloth slowly opened one eye.
"Monkey," he said. "If you're
so hard-working, you try
lifting Elephant's weights."

"Easy!" said Monkey,
and he tried to lift
the weights.
Elephant giggled as . . .

So Elephant tried to
jump on the trampoline.
Kangaroo laughed as . . .

CRASH!

. . . Elephant fell right through.
"Don't laugh at me, Kangaroo!"
said Elephant grumpily.
"Can *you* run like Cheetah?"

So Kangaroo tried
the treadmill.
Cheetah chuckled as
Kangaroo landed on . . .

. . . her bottom!

OOOOOOW!

"Cheetah!" said Kangaroo crossly. "If you're so clever, you swing like Monkey."

So Cheetah climbed
the high bars and
swung right into . . .

By now, everyone was very hot,
very tired, and very, very cross.

"This is useless," they muttered.
"Who caused all this trouble?"

"It wasn't me," said Cheetah.
"I was busy running."

"It wasn't me," said Kangaroo.
"I was busy bouncing."

"It wasn't me," said Elephant.
"I was busy lifting weights."

"And it wasn't me," said Monkey.
"I was busy swinging."

All the animals turned
and looked at . . .

SLOTH!

"Hey, Sloth," they called.
"You started this!"

Sloth turned lazily.
"You must see by now,"
he said. "We were all busy doing
what we do best. Even me!"

The animals thought about it.
"Yes!" they cried. "We're all good at
running or jumping or lifting or swinging.
But Sloth is the very best at . . .

"SNO

OZING!"

"Exactly!" said Sloth.
And with a stretch
and a yawn, he fell
fast asleep!